Principle W

- The Beavers' Dam
- Great Pine
- Grand Oak
- Stinky Stump
- Sweet Bunnies Burrow
- Summertime Blue Juicer Tree

oods

Busy Beaver Creek

Fallen Maple

The Magnolia Clearing

The Cave of Courage

The Honesty Tree

Blossom's Clubhouse

Hidden Pond

Dedicated to my mother, Helen Rench Stroner, for her unconditional love, support and encouragment

Principle Woods™ Celebrates Honesty

Author
Sandra Stroner Sivulich

Illustrator
Kevin Shore

Principle Woods, Inc.
One San Jose Place, Suite 11
Jacksonville, Florida 32257
www.principlewoods.com

This book is a work of fiction. Names, characters, places, and incidents either are products of the author's imagination or are used fictitiously. Any resemblance to actual events or locales or persons, living or dead, is entirely coincidental.

Text copyright © 2003 by Principle Woods, Inc.
Illustrations copyright © 2003 by Principle Woods, Inc.
All rights reserved. No part of this book may be used or reproduced in any manner without the prior written permission of Principle Woods, Inc.

Designed by David Whitlock, Principle Design Group, Inc.

Printed in Singapore

0203-01ED
ISBN 0-9719228-1-0

Contents

Story One
The Thank You Flowers 6

Story Two
I Can Do This! 32

Story Three
Truth or Trouble 50

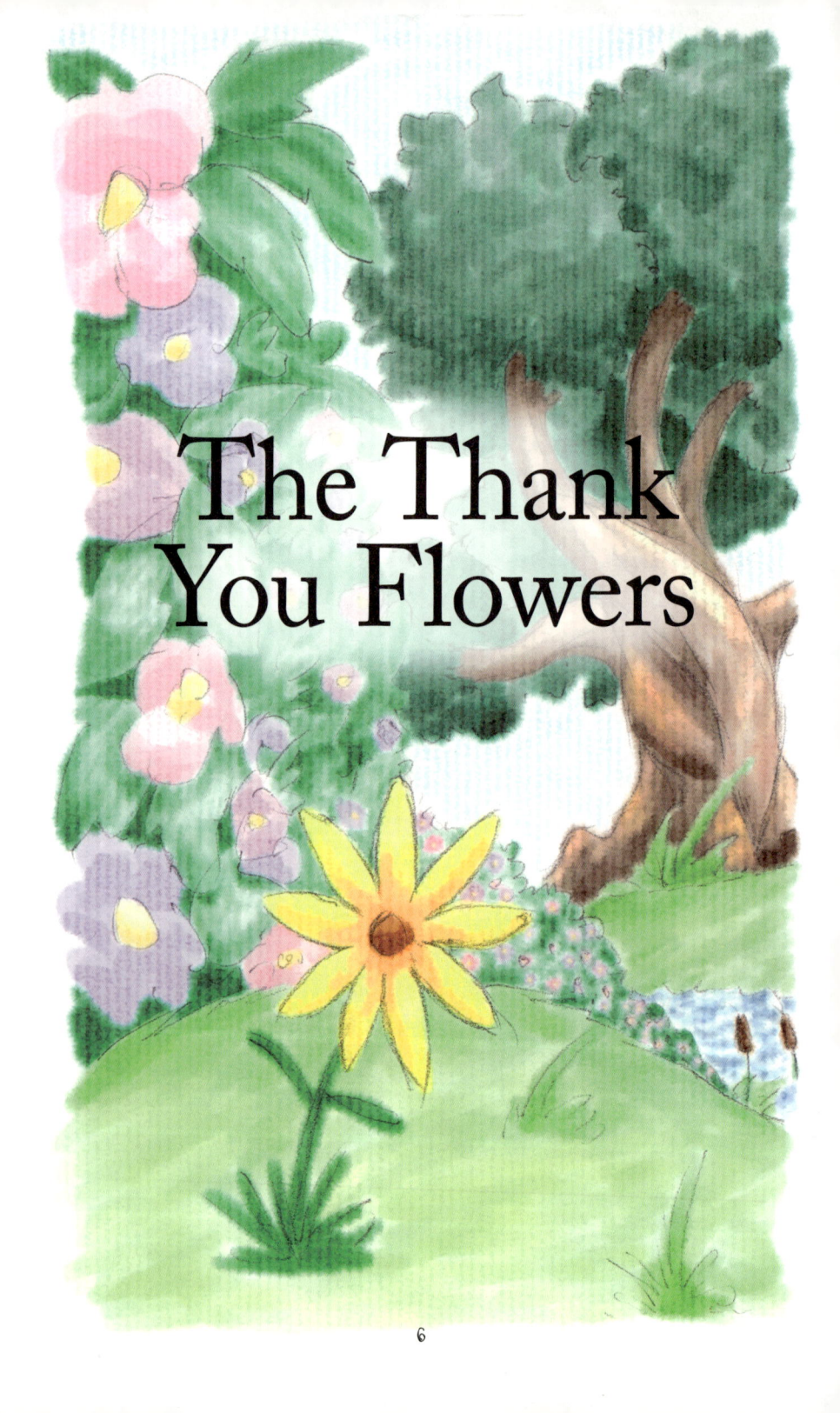

The Thank You Flowers

"I will pick a blue flower.

"I will pick a red flower.

"I will pick a yellow flower. And then I will pick more," Grinder, the beaver, sang as he waddled from flower to flower in the field near Busy Beaver Creek. "What pretty flowers I have picked! "

He was so happy that he could give the flowers as a thank you gift to his best friend, Chopsie. She had worked so hard building the new dam over Busy Beaver Creek. He wanted her to know how thankful he was for her hard work. He had told her thank you, but now the flowers would show her how he felt, too.

"She will be so happy with all the flowers I have picked for her," Grinder thought happily. "Picking flowers is hard work. I will take a little rest before I go home with the flowers," Grinder decided as he put the flowers down on the ground under a tree.

Blossom, the skunk, came walking along the path. She saw the flowers. She loved the blue flowers. She loved the red flowers. She loved the yellow flowers. She loved all the flowers.

She wanted the flowers. She wanted to take the flowers to her clubhouse. The flowers would look very pretty in her clubhouse.

She knew the flowers had to belong to someone. Then, she saw Grinder taking a nap. She looked at Grinder. She looked at the flowers. She told herself that it did not matter if the flowers belonged to Grinder.

She needed them. She wanted them. Besides, the blue, red, and yellow flowers were much too pretty for Grinder. Only a pretty skunk, like her, should have pretty flowers. Grinder did not have a clubhouse. She did. Grinder did not have parties. She did. Yes, those blue, red, and yellow flowers should be hers.

No one would see her taking the flowers. No one would ever know that she did. So, she took all the flowers in her arms and happily skipped home.

After she left, Grinder woke up. He looked around. Where were the flowers he picked?

He looked to the left. No flowers. He looked to the right. No flowers. He looked behind the tree. No flowers.

Grinder thought, "Maybe I just had a dream about the flowers. Maybe I didn't pick them at all." Grinder went home. He did not have a thank you gift for Chopsie. He was sad.

Blossom loved her blue, red, and yellow flowers. She wanted her friends to see her pretty flowers. She wanted them to tell her, "Oh, Blossom, those pretty flowers are just perfect for a pretty skunk." She decided she would have a party to show off her pretty flowers.

Blossom invited Burly, the bear.

Blossom invited Tipper, the squirrel.

Blossom invited Sage, the owl.

Blossom invited Springer, the bunny.

Blossom did not invite Grinder and Chopsie, the beavers, to come to her clubhouse for a party.

Everyone came to the party. They all loved the blue, red, and yellow flowers. They asked Blossom where she got such pretty flowers.

Blossom did not know what she should say. Blossom made up an answer. She told them Grinder gave them to her.

Tipper and Springer were mad because they did not get any flowers from Grinder. "Grinder must like you better than he likes us," they told Blossom.

Tipper and Springer left the clubhouse and marched over to Busy Beaver Creek. "We are mad at you because you did not give us pretty flowers. We just came from Blossom's party and she told us you gave her the pretty flowers. How come you like Blossom better than you like us?" they shouted at Grinder. Before Grinder could say a word, Tipper and Springer quickly turned around and left.

Poor Grinder. He did not understand why Tipper and Springer were mad at him. He did not understand why he and Chopsie were not invited to the party at the clubhouse.

The only thing he understood was that he was not happy. First, he was sad because he had no thank you gift for Chopsie. Next, he was sad because he was not invited to the party at the clubhouse. Finally, he was sad because his friends were mad at him. He did not know what to do.

He thought, "Blossom never wonders what to do. In fact, she always tells us what to do. I will go to the clubhouse and ask her why Tipper and Springer are mad at me. Then I will ask her about not being invited to her party."

Blossom was very surprised to see Grinder at her clubhouse. "What are you doing here?" she asked. "The party is over. Besides, you weren't even invited."

"I know I was not invited. I came to ask you to help me. I am very sad." He told her why he was sad.

Blossom did not know what to do now. She knew what she had done was wrong. She knew Grinder was sad because she had not been honest. She knew that one lie grew into more. She knew that by telling the truth she could stop Grinder from being sad.

It would be very hard to tell him about taking the blue, red, and yellow flowers. It would be very hard to tell everyone that she had done something wrong.

Maybe…she would not tell. After all, no one had seen her do it. There was no proof. Did it really matter if Grinder was sad? He would get over it.

Then she looked at the flowers. They were no longer pretty. They looked sad. Now Grinder was sad, too. Not being honest was making everything sad. She knew she had to fix what she had done.

"Grinder," said Blossom, "It is my fault that you are sad." She told him the truth.

She told him about taking the flowers. She told him why he was not invited to her party at the clubhouse. She told him what she had told their friends.

She told him she would pick more blue, red, and yellow flowers so he could give Chopsie her thank you gift. She told him she would explain what she had done to their friends.

Grinder was not mad at Blossom. He was glad that she had been honest. He was glad he could now understand what had happened.

But most of all, he was glad Chopsie would have her flowers!

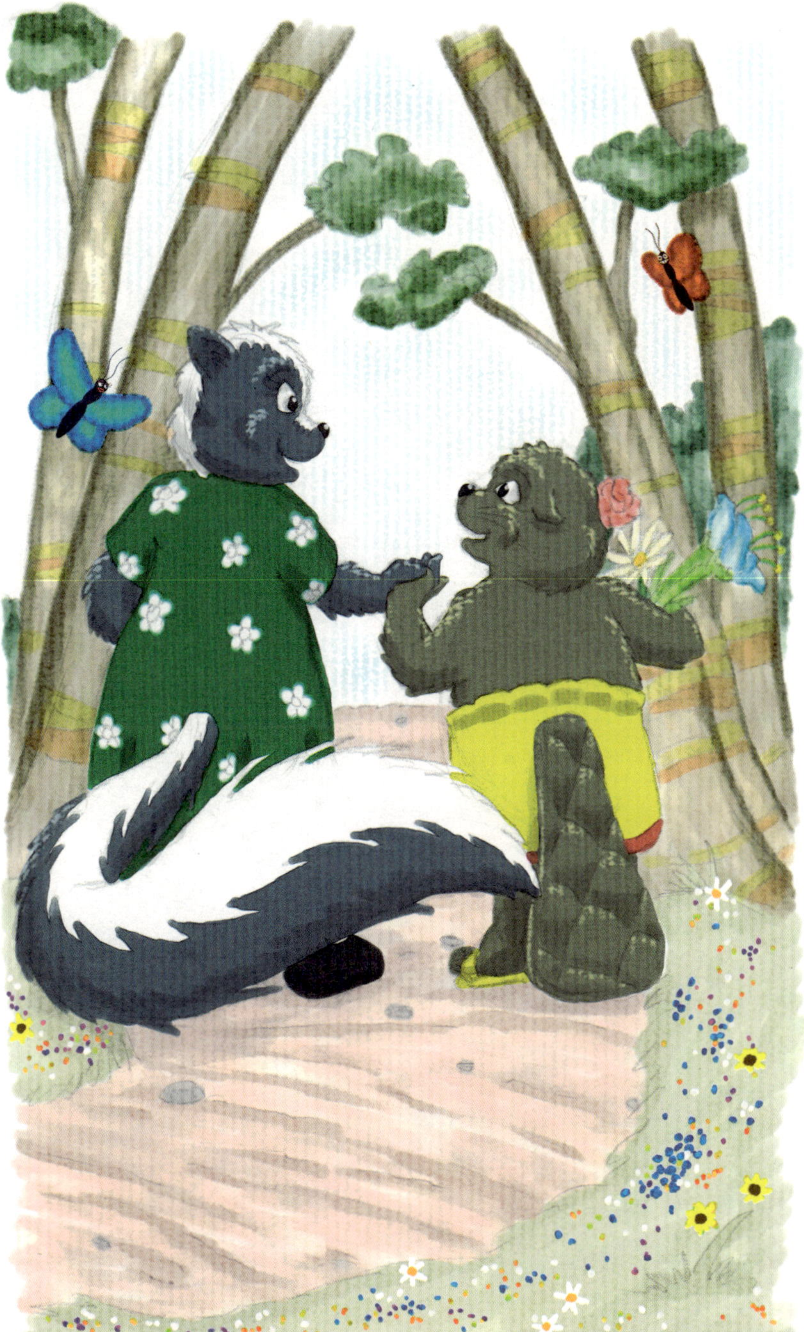

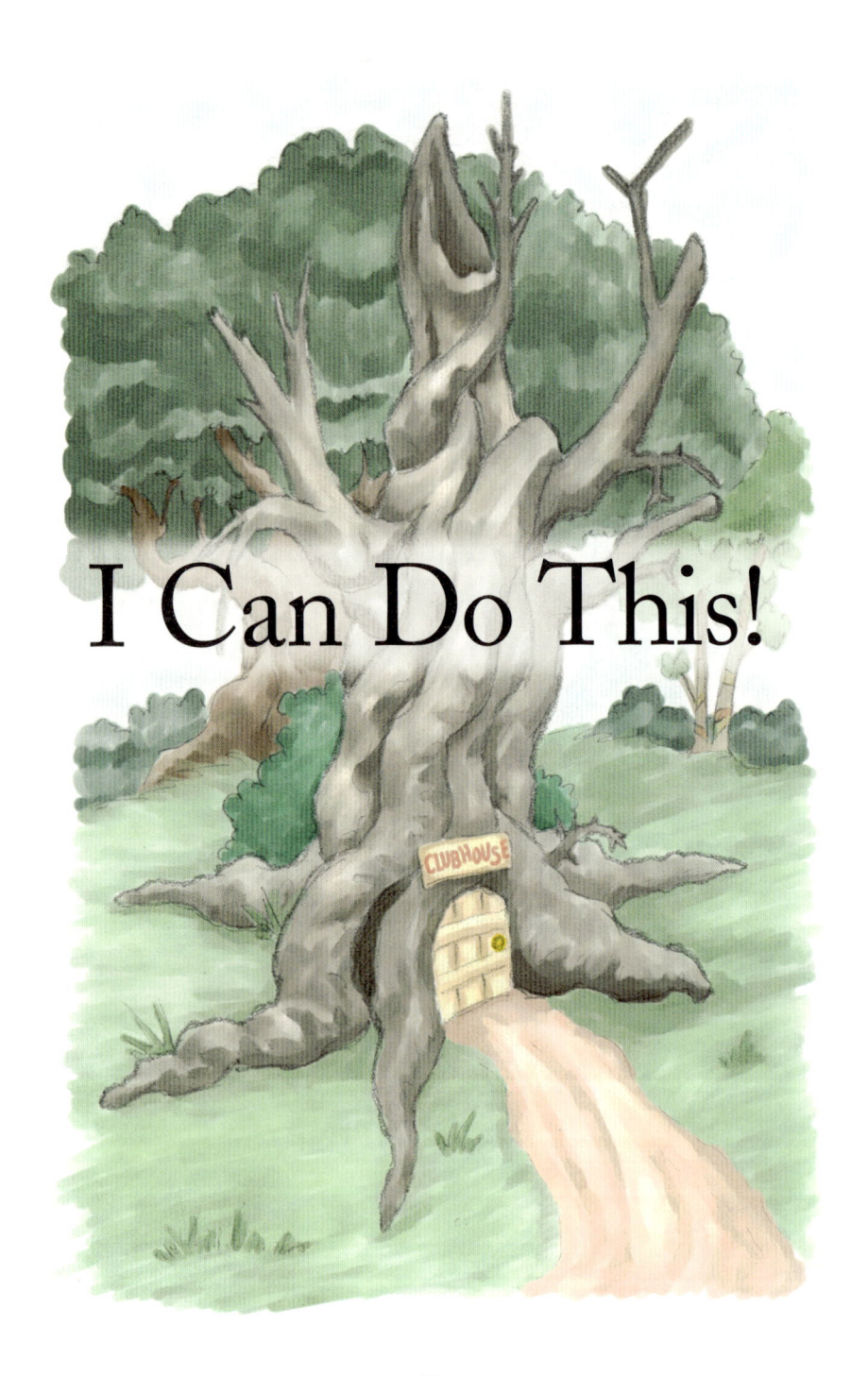

I Can Do This!

All the animals were at the clubhouse. They were playing the game, I Can Do This, to find out who could do the most things. Everyone was playing except Tipper, the squirrel. The other animals had asked Tipper to take a time-out because he could never wait for his turn. Now, he could only watch the others from the sidelines as they played.

"I can do this. I can roar," said Burly, the bear.

"One point," announced Grinder, the scorekeeper.

"I can do this. I can fly," said Sage, the owl.

"One point," announced Grinder, the scorekeeper.

"I can do this. I can hop," said Springer, the bunny.

"One point," announced Grinder, the scorekeeper.

"I can do this. I can chop," said Chopsie, the beaver.

"One point," announced Grinder, the scorekeeper.

"I wish I could roar, fly, hop, and chop. If I added those things to all the things I can really do, I really, truly would win. I'd show them!" Tipper said angrily as he kicked the dirt.

And then Tipper got an idea.

"What a great idea! I know what I can do to win once I'm back in the game. I will tell them that I can do everything they can do, BUT I'll say that I can only do it in the dark and when I am alone. Then no one can ever ask to see me roar, fly, hop, and chop. If they were there, I wouldn't be alone. If they were there, they couldn't see me because I'd be in the dark.

"Oh, how easy this is. Why didn't I ever think of doing this before? What a good idea I have had. I can keep making up things that I can do, but I never have to prove anything. Of course I will win because I will tell them I can do all they can do and more.

"Hello, my friends. I am ready to come back and play I Can Do This," Tipper called from the sidelines.

"Well, we hope you can wait for your turn this time," said Burly, the bear. "Welcome back. Let's play. I'll start. I can do this. I can roar."

Even before Grinder could announce the point, Tipper jumped in front of him and shouted, "I can roar, too." Burly just looked at Tipper and shook his head sadly.

Sage, the owl, got up next and said, "I can do this. I can fly."

Once again, Tipper jumped up and shouted, "I can fly, too." Sage just looked at Tipper and shook her head sadly.

Springer, the bunny, got up next and said, "I can do this. I can…" Even before he could finish, Tipper jumped up and shouted, "I can hop, too." Springer just looked at Tipper and shook his head sadly.

Chopsie, the beaver, got up next and said, "I can do this. I can chop." Tipper jumped in front of her and shouted, "I can chop, too."

Chopsie did not shake her head at him. Chopsie put her hand out and shouted, "Stop right where you are, Tipper! You cannot play any more. You cannot do all the things you are saying you can do. And besides, once again, you are not waiting for your turn."

All the animals joined in and yelled, "Tipper, you cannot roar, fly, hop, or chop. You are just making those things up. You can't play anymore."

Tipper stayed right where he was and yelled back, "You are all wrong. I am right. I can so roar, fly, hop, and chop. I can do all those things BUT no one can see me. The reason no one can see me is because I can only do those things in the dark and when I am alone. So there!

"Too bad, so sad that you don't believe me. If you don't want to play with me any more, I don't want to play with you either. Anyway, I win because I can do more things than all of you put together," and Tipper tossed his bushy tail in the air and started to go away.

"Please, stop and listen before you

leave," said Sage. "First of all, dear Tipper, if we were all the same and could do the same things, Principle Woods would be a very dull place, indeed. Each of us can do certain things better than anyone else. Only you can climb trees faster than any of us. Only you can hide berries and nuts so that no one else can find them. Only you can invent the best games and make us laugh because of your silly tricks.

"There has never been another Tipper. There will never be another Tipper. Just as there will never be another me or Burly or Springer. Of course, there can be animals with our same names and animals that look just like we do, BUT… each animal is different. Each animal is like a gift, because he is very, very special and nobody is exactly like him.

"Let's be honest when we play I Can Do This. Don't pretend to be somebody else. We like you just the way you are."

"Oh, no, we don't," said Chopsie. "We don't like it when he doesn't wait his turn to play the game."

Everyone laughed at Chopsie's honesty–especially Tipper.

Truth or Trouble

Chopsie, the beaver, invited all of her friends to Busy Beaver Creek. She wanted them to see the pretty things she could chop out of wood.

"Oh, Chopsie, I really love what you have made," exclaimed Blossom, the skunk. "Springer, don't you just love this piece of artwork?" asked Blossom.

Springer did not like it at all. He did not know what to say. He just smiled and said, "Yes, it is my favorite piece."

When Chopsie heard him say that, she was very happy. "Oh, Springer, I did not know you liked my work so much! I would like you to take it home with you so you can look at it all the time," said Chopsie.

Springer did not know what to do. The artwork scared him. Springer did not know what to say. He just smiled and took the piece of artwork.

The next day, Blossom invited all her friends to her clubhouse. "Hello, hello, hello, all my friends. I am so happy that you could come. Today I have made a special treat for all of you to eat. I call it Blossom Berry Pie. Please try some," said Blossom as she sliced the pie and put a piece on everyone's plate.

Everyone ate it. Everyone liked it. Everyone, that is except Springer. He did not like Blossom Berry Pie. He did not like it at all. He did not know what to do with it. He did not want to tell Blossom that he did not like her food. So, he picked up his plate and slowly walked outside and hid his Blossom Berry Pie behind a tree.

When he returned, Blossom saw his empty plate. "Oh, Springer, you must really love Blossom Berry Pie! Your plate is empty. Here, have another piece," insisted Blossom.

Springer could not tell Blossom the truth. He just smiled and put out his plate. "In fact, because you like my pie so much," said Blossom, "I'm going to give the rest of it to you to take home!" Springer did not know what to say. He just smiled and put out his plate.

As Springer stood there with his full plate, Tipper, the squirrel, came over to see him. "Springer, my friend, I have an idea. You and I are going to catch butterflies and start a butterfly zoo."

Springer did not want to catch butterflies and put them in a zoo. He did not know what to do. He did not want to make Tipper mad by saying no to him. So he just smiled and followed Tipper.

"Now hear this, now hear this!" Tipper announced to their friends. "Springer and I are going to catch butterflies and start a butterfly zoo."

When the other animals heard that, they said, "Shame on you for hunting the poor, little butterflies! Butterflies should be free! How would you like it if someone hunted you and put you in a zoo? If you do that, you are no longer our friends."

"Too bad, so sad," said Tipper. "Come on, Springer. Let's go home so we can get an early start for the hunt in the morning."

When Springer arrived at Sweet Bunnies Burrow, he was not happy. First of all, he did not want to look at Chopsie's artwork. It scared him. Next, he was hungry but did not want to eat Blossom Berry Pie. Finally, his friends were mad at him for hunting butterflies. All this happened because he was not honest with his friends. He did not know what to do.

The next day, Sage, the wise owl, saw the sad bunny and flew down to help him. After hearing what happened, she said, "Dear, sweet Springer, if you don't like something, you must be honest and say so. Do not say you like something just to make the other animals happy. Now, bring along the Blossom Berry Pie and the artwork, and come with me to the clubhouse."

When they arrived at the clubhouse, Springer told everyone, "I have learned it is best to be honest and tell the truth.

"So, Chopsie, please take your artwork back.

"Blossom, please share your pie with someone else.

"Tipper, please don't ask me to hunt butterflies."

The animals cheered.

Blossom said, "You saved the day. I didn't know what we'd eat today. Now, we can have Blossom Berry Pie."

Chopsie said, "I wanted my artwork back anyway. It belongs at Busy Beaver Creek. Thank you."

Tipper said, "That's okay, Springer. I changed my mind about the butterfly zoo anyway. I have an even better idea. Wait until you hear!"

Burly said, "Tipper, I think we can all wait awhile to hear about your new idea. We are glad you are no longer hunting butterflies. All animals should be free—free to move about, free to have their own opinions and free to honestly say what they think!"